HELLO, I'm THEA!

I'm *Geronimo Stilton*'s sister. As I'm sure you know from my brother's bestselling novels, I'm a special correspondent for *The Rodent's Gazette*, Mouse Island's most famouse newspaper. Unlike my 'fraidy mouse brother, I absolutely adore traveling, having adventures, and meeting rodents from all around the world!

The adventure I want to tell you about begins at Mouseford Academy, the school I went to when I was a young mouseling. I had such a great experience there as a student that I came back to teach a journalism class.

When I returned as a grown mouse, I met five really special students: Colette, Nicky, Pamela, Paulina, and Violet. You could hardly imagine five more different mouselings, but they became great friends right away. And they liked me so much that they decided to name their group after me: the Thea Sisters! I was so touched by that, I decided to write about their adventures. So turn the page to read a fabumouse adventure about the

THEA SISTERS!

Colette

She has a passion for clothing and style, especially anything pink. When she grows up, she wants to be a fashion editor.

Paulina

Cheerful and kind, she loves traveling and meeting rodents from all over the world. She has a magic touch when it comes to technology.

Violet

She's the bookworm of the group, and she loves learning. She enjoys classical music and dreams of becoming a famouse violinist.

THE THEA SISTERS

Nicky

She comes from Australia and is very enthusiastic about sports and nature. She loves being outside and is always ready to get up and go!

Pamela

She is a great mechanic: Give her a screwdriver and she'll fix anything! She loves pizza, which she eats every day, and she loves to cook.

Do you want to help the Thea Sisters in this new adventure? It's not hard — just follow the clues!

When you see this magnifying glass, pay attention: It means there's an important clue on the page. Each time one appears, we'll review the clues so we don't miss anything.

**ARE YOU READY?
A NEW MYSTERY AWAITS!**

AND THE
RACE FOR THE
GOLD

Scholastic Inc.

Published by Scholastic Inc., *Publishers since 1920,* 557 Broadway, New York, NY 10012. SCHOLASTIC and associated logos are trademarks and/or registered trademarks of Scholastic Inc.

ISBN 978-1-338-58749-4

Text by Thea Stilton
Original title *Sognando le Olimpiadi*
Cover by Iacopo Bruno (art director), Valeria Brambilla, and Flavio Ferron
Illustrations by Barbara Pellizzari, Chiara Balleello, Alessandro Muscillo, and Valentina Grassini
Graphics by Giovanna Ferraris/theWorldofDOT and Chiara Cebraro

Special thanks to AnnMarie Anderson
Translated by Andrea Schaffer
Interior design by Becky James

10 9 8 7 6 5 4 3 2 1   20 21 22 23 24

Printed in the U.S.A.   40
First printing 2020

THE COLORS OF SUMMER

The Thea Sisters were enjoying a **perfect** breakfast at the beginning of a busy day: fresh-squeezed orange juice, toasted croissants, and good conversation! The end of the term was approaching *quickly*, and for the past few weeks, the five mice had been spending every spare minute preparing for their final **exams**. The friends were eagerly anticipating the long summer break in sight once they completed their **exams**.

"I don't know about the rest of you, but I could

really use a break from all this **studying**," Nicky announced. "What if we all plan to meet up later today for a non-study session?"

"I'm in!" Pamela agreed immediately. "I'm heading to the library to focus on my **history** paper, but I should be done soon."

"Colette and I have to **finish** our science project," Violet said.

"That's true, but if we get to work right now, we should be done in a few hours," Colette said eagerly.

"I'm off to a **computer science** study session now, but I'll head to our usual spot as soon as it's over," Paulina said. "See you all in the garden later?"

The Thea Sisters all nodded enthusiastically and headed off in **DIFFERENT** directions.

Later, the five mice were hard at work studying, writing, and researching when their cell phones all buzzed at the exact same time. The same message appeared on each screen:

> "These three colors wave to give you a clue.
> To a summer of sports: green, yellow, and blue!"

Pamela, Nicky, Colette, Violet, and Paulina all glanced down at their phones in confusion. None of them understood the **strange** message.

When the five friends gathered in the garden later that afternoon, they were all thinking about the message.

"I got a very **strange** text message!" Pamela exclaimed.

"That's strange, me, too," Violet said. "I think it's a riddle."

"I got it, too," Nicky added. "I didn't recognize the number. It's definitely some sort of puzzle."

"GREEN, YELLOW, and BLUE," reflected Paulina aloud. "The colors must mean something . . ."

"And it said something about sports and the summer," Paulina added.

"Well, I've been thinking," Paulina said. "What if the colors are from a FLAG?" She tapped out something on her tablet and then showed the results to her friends. "It could be the Brazilian flag."

"Of course!" Nicky exclaimed enthusiastically. "The Mouselympics will be in Brazil this summer!

The message has to have something to do with that."

"Yes, but what about the Mouselympics?" Pamela wondered, trying to put together the pieces of the puzzle.

The friends were quiet for a minute as they all thought hard about

Of course!

the RIDDLE. Then all at once, they each came to the same conclusion.

"It must be *Beatrice Oliveira*!" Violet shouted suddenly. "She loves sports lives in Brazil — the message must be from her!"

The others nodded in agreement.

"Yes, definitely," Colette agreed, a smile spreading across her snout.

At that moment, Paulina's phone rang: It was a video call from the mouse who had sent the mysterimouse message!

The Thea Sisters hurried to gather around Paulina so they could all fit in the screen. A familiar snout smiled back at them.

"Bea!" Paulina exclaimed happily. "It's good to hear from you!"

"We were right," Nicky said, and her friends laughed.

"We put the clues together and knew that

message had to be from you," Violet added.

"Hi!" Beatrice replied. "I knew you'd figure it out. After all, you're the Thea Sisters, the best **detectives** on Whale Island!"

AN UNEXPECTED INVITATION

The Thea Sisters hadn't seen their friend Beatrice in more than a year, but when her smiling snout appeared on the screen, it was as if no **time** had passed. In an instant, the five friends recalled many memories of their time with Beatrice. She had visited Mouseford Academy from Rio de Janeiro to participate in a track-and-field competition, along with students from all over the **world**.

The Thea Sisters had become fast friends with Beatrice, who was smart, funny, and an excellent athlete. Paulina, Colette, Pam, Nicky, and

Violet spent a lot of time with their Brazilian friend, showing her around Whale Island and cheering her to **victory**.

"This isn't your phone number," Paulina pointed out. "Admit it, you trickster: You used another phone on purpose so we wouldn't know it was you!"

Beatrice laughed. "Okay, okay, you're right," she admitted. "I borrowed a cell phone from a friend to **surprise** you. It was more **fun** that way!"

"You are such a sneaky mouse!" Colette said.

"It's great to hear from you," Nicky said. "You must be so **excited** about the Mouselympic Games!"

"Yes," Beatrice agreed. "Everymouse in Rio is excited."

"Tell us everything!" Pam said eagerly. "What is your city doing to get ready for the **BIG** event?"

"I have a lot to tell you," Beatrice said. "And I promise to update you every **NIGHT** during the Games."

"Terrific," Colette agreed. "That sounds like a great plan!"

Beatrice smiled mysteriously. "Maybe we can even do it while we **munch** on Brazilian cookies together!"

Colette looked at her friends in **confusion**. Bea had introduced them to her favorite crunchy, doughnut-shaped cookies, which she had brought with her from Rio de Janeiro the previous year. But Colette didn't know anyone who **SOLD** them on Whale Island.

"Probably not," Pamela said sadly. "I don't think it will be easy for us to find them. Maybe you can send us a box!"

Beatrice broke into a wide grin, her eyes **sparkling**.

"You'll have plenty of them if you come visit me in Rio de Janeiro!" she burst out excitedly. "That's why I called! I wanted to invite the five of you to spend the summer here with me and my family. We can enjoy the Mouselympics together!"

"Wow!" Violet said without hesitation. "That would be *wonderful*! We can meet you in Brazil when we finish our exams."

The mouselets nodded in agreement.

"Perfect!" Bea said. "I have to get to practice. But I am so excited to see you all soon."

Paulina ended the call and the five friends began *chattering* excitedly.

"I had no idea our study **break** was going to transform into a travel-planning session!" Colette exclaimed.

"Yes, what an excellent **surprise**," Pam agreed.

"Now, what do you say we all get back to work?" Violet suggested.

"Definitely," Nicky agreed. "I can barely focus, but the sooner we finish our school projects and exams, the sooner we can plan our trip. I'm so excited. **BRAZIL AWAITS US!**"

WELCOME TO BRAZIL!

Brazil is the largest country in South America and the fifth-largest country in the world.

One-third of the world's rain forests are found in Brazil, and the country has the biggest variety of animals in the world.

Brasília is the capital of Brazil, while Rio de Janeiro is known for its beautiful beaches. Every winter, Rio de Janeiro holds its famouse Carnaval do Rio de Janeiro, a boisterous and colorful holiday that attracts tourists from every part of the world!

A MAGNIFICENT SUMMER

The week **after** Beatrice's invitation passed quickly.

Colette, Pamela, Paulina, Nicky, and Violet continued to **STUDY** hard for their exams. Finally, it was the last day of the school term!

"AND WE'RE DONE!" Nicky exclaimed as she exited the classroom where she and her friends had just finished their science exam.

The Thea Sisters high-fived one another

and hurried back to their rooms.

"I'm so excited for summer!" Pam cheered happily.

In between study sessions, the five friends had managed to plan and organize their trip to Brazil. They had done a lot of research and had chosen a *FLIGHT* from Whale Island that would take them directly to **Rio de Janeiro**. Their vacation was about to begin, and all they had to do was pack their bags and head for the airport!

Colette dashed around her room, pulling clothes out of her closet and tossing them into her suitcase.

"Are you almost done, Coco?" Pam asked her friend. "Our flight **leaves** in just a few hours!"

17

"Yes, I know," Colette replied. "Do you think I should **bring** this jacket?"

"Maybe if you were going to Alaska!" Pam joked. "It's going to be warm in Brazil."

"I know," Colette sighed. "But when I pack for a trip, I always worry I'll leave something important behind."

Nicky poked her snout into the room.

"Are you ready?" she asked as she pointed at the clock. "We have to leave for the airport right away or we'll be **late**!"

"Okay, okay," Colette said as she closed her suitcase and put on her backpack. "If I forgot something, I guess I'll just have to go shopping in Brazil!"

The five friends grabbed their bags and hurried to the airport.

The flight was long, but when they saw the eastern coast of Brazil and the golden beaches of **Rio de Janeiro** outside the airplane window, the Thea Sisters were breathless with excitement!

Between the Atlantic Ocean and the lush, green mountains that overlooked the city, the mouselets could just see the towering skyscrapers of the enormouse **METROPOLIS**.

"Wow!" Paulina exclaimed as she followed her friends off the plane. "I can't believe we're finally here!"

Paulina had been born and raised in nearby Peru, so to her, even the smell of the air reminded her of home!

"We landed **RIGHT** on time!" Pam said happily. "Bea should already be here."

The Thea Sisters only had to turn a corner

before Beatrice appeared in front of them, a smile spreading across her snout.

"*Bem-vindas*," Bea said, rushing to **hug** her friends. "Welcome!"

"*Obrigada*," Violet replied. She had learned how to say *thank you*, along with a few other phrases, in Portuguese before their trip.

"It's **great** to see you again!" Bea exclaimed. Then she ushered them outside to a waiting taxi. The driver took them to the Ipanema neighborhood, where Beatrice lived with her **family**.

"Here is my home!" Beatrice said proudly as she showed them inside an apartment that looked out over one of Rio's most *beautiful* beaches.

"My parents are expecting us for dinner at their *churrascaria,* but we have some time to stop at the beach first!"

A CHURRASCARIA is a typical Brazilian restaurant where you can eat *churrasco,* or meat that has been cooked on a skewer over a grill.

"Yes!" cheered Nicky. "I've been looking forward to seeing the sea since we landed!"

"Well, we actually already saw it from the window of the plane, but it will be even better seeing it from the ground!" Paulina said.

"Then let's go!" Bea said.

The six friends headed to the beach and Colette looked out at the crystal blue water and sighed happily.

"This summer will be *great*!" she said.

"I think so, too!" Pam agreed.

Meanwhile, Nicky headed straight for the ocean, where she happily dipped her paws in the surf.

"Something tells me it's going to be **hard** to convince Nicky to go back to Mouseford after this trip," Violet added with a laugh.

A TOAST TO BRAZIL!

"Beatrice!" "Bea!" "Hi!"

A chorus of cheerful voices cried out in the distance. The Thea Sisters tried to shade their eyes from the sun as they looked down the beach to see who was calling out to their friend. Three figures were RUNNING toward them, waving their arms. Bea waved back, and when the three mice reached the group, Beatrice introduced them.

"Colette, Pamela, Paulina, Violet, and Nicky, I want you to meet Fernanda, Vera, and Luiza, the other three members of my **relay team**!"

"Beatrice has told us so much about you!" Vera exclaimed.

"We're so happy to finally meet you!" Fernanda added.

"What do you say we all go get a **cool** drink together?" Luiza proposed.

"But we're in the middle of a training run," Fernanda protested. "We can't **STOP** now!"

"Oh, lighten up a bit," Vera **JOKED**. "It will be a good chance to rest for a while between workouts."

These are my teammates!

Beatrice!

Hi!

"Vera's right," Luiza said, smiling. "A short break would be good for us. And I know a place nearby that will be perfect!"

Luiza led the group to a little wooden kiosk on the beach. There were small tables, covered by umbrellas, overlooking the sea. Plenty of sunbathers and swimmers sat having drinks and enjoying some shade.

"What a great idea!" Pamela said happily as she took a sip of her juice. "This really hits the spot. And what an amazing view!"

"Mmmm, yes," Colette said as she sipped her juice. "It's nice to sit down for a minute after our day of traveling. And this juice is so refreshing!"

Fernanda had been quiet until that moment. But now she looked at Bea intensely.

"When we're done here, you'll come train with us, right?"

"Um, well . . ." Bea replied, hesitating. "Today I'm spending time with my friends. We have plans to meet my parents at their churrascaria."

"But you can't skip a day of training!" Fernanda replied, **GLARING** at Bea. "Don't you want to qualify?"

"Qualify for what?" Nicky asked, curious.

"The Mouselympics," Beatrice squeaked with a heavy sigh. She looked uncomfortable. "Our **TRAINER** says the four of us have a good chance of making the **Brazilian** Mouselympic team!"

Qualify for what?

"Our Beatrice is a real sprinter!" Vera said enthusiastically. "If she runs the last leg of the **relay**, we might really be able to do it!"

"**WOW**, the Mouseleympic team!" Paulina cheered. "That's fantastic! Why didn't you say something earlier?"

Fantastic!

Beatrice smiled, looking a little embarrassed. "I was going to tell you. I was waiting for the right **moment**."

"How exciting for you!" Violet said.

"Yes, I know," Bea replied, but she looked worried. "It's an *incredible* opportunity."

Pam raised her glass.

"A toast!" she said happily. "Here's to Beatrice, here's to Brazil, and here's to the **MOUSELYMPICS**!"

While the friends clinked their glasses together and began chattering *excitedly*,

Colette's gaze settled on Bea. Something didn't **ADD UP**: Her friend's snout looked happy, but her eyes said something else entirely.

WHAT IS A RELAY?

A relay is a team running competition in which each athlete runs part of the race, which is called a leg. Each team carries an aluminum cylinder called a baton, which is passed from one runner to the next in a precise exchange zone called the changeover box.

In the 4x100 relay, four athletes run 100 meters each, for a total of 400 meters. In the 4x400 relay, four athletes run 400 meters each, for a total of 1,600 meters. The athlete who is receiving the baton gets into position and begins to run, trying to match the speed of the current runner. If the baton is passed outside the changeover box, the team is disqualified from the race.

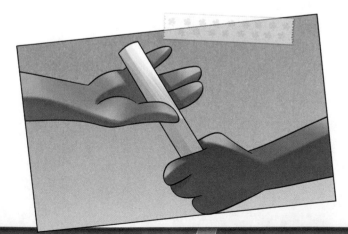

MEETING THE FAMILY

Beatrice and the Thea Sisters said good-bye and headed toward the **CHURRASCARIA**.

Colette noticed that ever since the topic of qualifying for the Mouselympics had come up, something in Beatrice had **changed**. She still tried to be cheerful, but her eyes looked sad.

"Is everything okay?" Colette asked gently.

"Yes, I'm fine," Bea said.

Colette glanced at her friends, a worried look on her snout. She could tell that her friends were **CONCERNED**, too.

But the Thea Sisters all seemed to understand that Bea didn't want to talk about whatever was bothering her.

"We're here to **support** you," Paulina said, putting her paw around Bea's shoulders.

"Yes, and if your team qualifies for the Mouselympics, you know we'll be at every race!" Nicky added.

"Thank you," Bea said, smiling. "But we still don't know if we'll qualify for the team. There are so many talented athletes with the same **dream**!"

"Of course," Violet said. "But you four have a chance!"

"Here we are!" Beatrice said brightly as they arrived at the churrascaria. She seemed **eager** to change the subject. "My parents will be so excited to meet you. Let's go in!"

The churrascaria was on the ground floor of a short, mustard yellow–colored building. The buildings around it sparkled in every shade of **RED**, **BLUE**, and **YELLOW**.

"I just love the **colors** in this city," Violet gushed to Bea.

"Yes, they're so beautiful," Colette agreed.

As the mice stepped into the churrascaria, they realized the cheerful bursts of color continued inside, from the walls and floor to the tablecloths and brightly colored paintings hanging on the walls.

Two adorable ratlets dressed in matching clothes scampered up to the group.

"Hi!" the first ratlet exclaimed.

"You must be the friends Beatrice invited to visit us!" said the second.

"These are my brothers, Tiago and Felipe," Beatrice explained. "In case you couldn't tell, they're **TWINS!**"

"I'm Ricardo, and this is Juliana," said another mouse as he stepped out from behind the counter and pointed to a mouse who looked just like Beatrice. "We're Beatrice's parents. We're happy to have you as our guests. Beatrice has told us wonderful things about you."

Hi!

"Thank you for having us!" Pamela replied on behalf of herself and her friends. "We're thrilled to be spending time in Rio de Janeiro."

"Maybe we'll even get to see Beatrice **compete** in the Mouselympics while we're here!" Nicky added.

When he heard Nicky's words, Ricardo's snout darkened. He turned to his daughter.

"Bea, I thought we spoke about this," he said sternly. "I don't want to hear any more talk about the **relay** and qualifying for the Mouselympics!"

"I know," Beatrice replied, looking sad. "I'm not spending any more time on sports than before. Don't worry."

"Our Beatrice has plans to become a doctor," Juliana explained to the Thea Sisters. "She needs to pay attention to her studies instead of being distracted by sports."

Colette looked at her friends. At last she understood the problem: Beatrice didn't

want to give up her **dream** of qualifying for the Mouselympics, but she also didn't want to **disappoint** her parents!

BREAKFAST ON THE BEACH

After dinner, the Thea Sisters headed back to Beatrice's home. Ricardo and Juliana had given the Thea Sisters a small but **comfortable** room in their apartment. It had five beds that had been made with cheerful colored sheets. Some **stools** served as nightstands, and on each one there was a small lamp and some orange candies. It was like a big slumber party!

The Thea Sisters **felt** right at home and settled down to sleep.

"The exam," Pamela mumbled in her sleep. "I'm going to be late for class!"

At the sound of their friend, the other Thea Sisters woke up.

Colette heard Pam muttering and realized her friend was dreaming.

"Don't **worry**, Pam," Colette said as she got out of bed and lifted the window shade. "We finished our exams a few days ago. Now we're on **Vacation**!"

Pam **rubbed** her eyes and sat up. "I slept so well I thought I was still at school!"

"I wonder if Beatrice is awake

Good morning!

The exam...

We're in Rio, Pam!

Ha, ha, ha!

Zzzzz...

yet," Paulina said as she glanced at the time on her cell phone. "It's still early."

"I'll go **SEE**," Violet offered. A minute later she returned with a note from Beatrice.

"There's no one home," Violet explained. "Ricardo and Juliana are probably working."

"Let's meet Bea at the library," Nicky suggested.

The others quickly got ready. Thanks to a map of the city that Beatrice had given them

I'm going out early to study and take Felipe and Tiago to kindergarten. If I'm not there when you wake, meet me at the library so we can have breakfast together!

—Bea

as soon as they'd arrived in Rio, they found the library quickly.

"There she is!" Pamela said, pointing at their **friend**. Beatrice was sitting behind a pile of books, so absorbed that she didn't realize they had arrived.

The Thea Sisters **APPROACHED** quietly so they wouldn't disturb the other students.

"Good morning!" Bea whispered when she finally saw them. "I thought you'd sleep in on your vacation. You're up early!"

"Not as early as you were!" Paulina said. "You must have started your day before DAWN!"

Bea nodded. "It's the only way to get everything done," she said. "Especially since we are training harder now."

"So you do want to try out for the MOUSELYMPIC team, then?" Nicky asked.

Beatrice nodded seriously. "It's a huge **opportunity**, and I don't want to miss it," she explained. "But I don't want to disappoint my parents, either. So I have to do everything possible to make sure my grades don't slip."

"You can do it!" Colette encouraged her. "You're bright and dedicated and a great athlete. And you work harder than any mouse I know!"

"Squeaking of working hard, you need a break!" Pamela reminded her. "Didn't you say something about breakfast?"

Beatrice laughed. "You're right," she said. "I have everything we need for the perfect picnic breakfast!"

Beatrice returned her books to the shelves, and she and the Thea Sisters left the library and headed toward the beach.

When they were all seated in the SHADE of the palm trees, Beatrice opened her backpack and took out her breakfast supplies: fruit juice, coconut water, yogurt, dried and fresh fruit, nuts, and cereal bars.

"I have TRAINING in a little bit," Beatrice

explained. "Every morning, I take the twins to kindergarten and then head to the library to study for a couple of hours before I meet up with my teammates."

"We can help you," Pamela offered as she **munched** on a cereal bar.

"That would be **GREAT**!" Bea replied enthusiastically. "Thank you!"

"This yogurt is so **good**!" Colette said. She had followed Beatrice's advice and added a little dried fruit, hazelnuts, and **honey** to her yogurt.

"This is my favorite breakfast to have on training days," Bea said cheerfully. "It's healthy and gives me plenty of energy for *RUNNING*!"

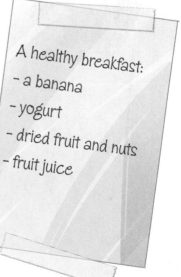

A healthy breakfast:
- a banana
- yogurt
- dried fruit and nuts
- fruit juice

"Well, I think it's perfect for spectators, too." Pam said, smiling. "Hand me another one. It takes a lot of energy to cheer for your friends!"

Yum!

A THOUSAND THINGS TO DO!

It was only ten in the morning, but with all the things Beatrice had already done, her day was well under way. Bea's life was full of commitments — she was a dedicated **student**, a promising ATHLETE, and a devoted big sister. Yet, she never seemed tired! Bea put her whole **heart** into everything she did.

Let's go!

"This is where I train every day," Beatrice said as she led her friends through the gate that encircled the running track. "It's like a **second** home to me. Actually, you could call it a **THIRD** home with all the time I spend at the **UNIVERSITY**!"

The Thea Sisters followed Bea across a manicured **GREEN FIELD** in the middle of an oval track. Bea showed them the stands where spectators could watch the training practice.

"Beatrice!" A young mouse ran up to meet them. "You're late!"

You're late!

"I'm sorry, Paulo!" Bea replied. "My friends are visiting, and I **lost** track of time . . ."

"The Mouselympic trials are coming up," the mouse replied. Judging by the whistle that he wore around his neck, he had to be Beatrice's coach. "We don't have a moment to lose if we want to qualify!

"Your teammates are already warming up," the coach continued. "Join them so we can begin."

"If we aren't any trouble, we would love to stay and **WATCH** from the stands," Nicky told Paulo.

"Of course!" the coach replied with a quick smile. "Support from friends is important!"

It was the first time that the Thea Sisters had watched a relay race practice, and they were very curious.

After they had warmed up, Bea and her teammates began practicing their baton handoff. The Thea Sisters watched in awe as the four mice sprinted around the track at incredible *SPEEDS.*

"It's impressive," Violet said. "They are so in sync with each other and they make it look

easy! But I'm sure they've practiced long and hard to make that magic happen."

The time **flew** by as the Thea Sisters watched Beatrice, Fernanda, Vera, and Luiza train.

When the four tired mice finally stepped off the track, the Thea Sisters dashed up to them.

"That was *fantastic*!" Violet told Bea.

Your turn!

"You're all amazing!" Colette added.

"Amazing, but not yet perfect," Paulo interjected. "We still have a lot of work to do. In the coming weeks, we will need to practice even more."

"B-but . . ." Beatrice said hesitantly. "I have to study, and my family . . . I don't know if I can do more . . ."

"We all have things to do, but this is important!" Fernanda snapped, a scowl on her snout. "You'll have to find a way to make it work."

"I'll do what I can," Beatrice replied, a worried look on her snout. Then she turned to the Thea Sisters. "I have to get to class. Do you want to come with me?"

Find a way!

The five friends accompanied

Bea to her lessons, and then to pick up the **TWINS** from kindergarten. After that, Beatrice had to head straight to the churrascaria, where she was filling in for a waitress who had called in **sick**.

"I can't believe how busy Beatrice is," Pamela said as she watched her friend scurry around the restaurant. "She never seems to have a **second** to rest!"

Let's get to work!

Suddenly, Colette had a realization.

"Yes, Bea has a full and **busy** life, but we can help!"

As soon as she said this, Colette went up to the counter and pulled out five clean aprons. She gave one to each of her friends.

"Come on, **let's get to work**!"

"What are you doing?" Beatrice asked with surprise as Paulina approached a table of guests.

"We'Re HeLPinG a fRienD!"

Paulina replied with a smile.

THE MISSING BAG

The Thea Sisters enjoyed their days sightseeing around **Rio de Janeiro**. As they strolled the streets of the vibrant city, the five friends had the constant feeling of finding themselves in a **colorful** and festive painting.

Whenever they could, the Thea Sisters helped Bea with her many responsibilities. But they also found time to explore the city. And so, one morning while Bea was in class, the five **friends** decided to take a cable car to the top of **Sugarloaf Mountain**.

From the top, they would have a **panoramic** view of Rio, Guanabara Bay, the city of Niterói, and the Atlantic Ocean.

The view was breathtaking, and the Thea Sisters soaked it in.

"This city seems more spectacular every day!" Violet said. "I want to **photograph** every angle!"

"That would be nice, but we really should head back," Colette said after glancing at the clock. "Beatrice is about to get out of class. If we want to help with her training, we need to **GO**!"

Once they got off the cable car, the Thea Sisters took the bus to the track. **Rio de Janeiro** is a big city, but little by little, they were figuring out how to navigate the streets. By the end of the **summer**, they would feel right at **HOME**!

What a magnificent city!

When they arrived at the track, Bea, Fernanda, Vera, and Luiza were already warming up.

"Hi!" Bea greeted them with a smile as she put down her jump rope. "How was your trip to Sugarloaf?"

"Beautiful!" Violet replied. "We took the cable car and had a *fantastic* view from the top."

"We had fun, but we missed you!" Colette added.

Nicky looked around the track and then glanced at her watch. Practice was running late, which was unusual.

"Why haven't you **started**?" Nicky asked, curious.

"Paulo isn't here yet," Vera responded. "He's usually **on time**."

"Here he is!" Fernanda exclaimed as Paulo

emerged from the locker room and jogged toward them.

"The batons!" Paulo squeaked, catching his breath. "They're MISSING!"

"What do you mean?" Violet asked.

Paulo explained that every night after practice, the batons were stored in a bag that was secured in a locker in the locker room.

"Yesterday I put them away," Beatrice confirmed. "I locked the locker just like always."

"Bea, are you sure?" Paulo asked. "Because the lock has disappeared along with the bag of batons!"

Bea looked shocked. "Of course I'm sure!" she squeaked.

"Who knows the **combination** to open the lock?" Violet asked.

Paulo thought for a moment.

Where are the batons?

"Just the five of us — me, Bea, Fernanda, Vera, and Luiza. But it's a **simple** combination — 4400, like the relay race. I didn't think anyone would be **interested** in stealing a bag of batons!"

"It does seem like a strange thing to steal," Paulina agreed. "The batons aren't worth a lot of money."

"Maybe you **accidentally** put in the wrong combination and the locker was left open, Bea," Colette suggested. "That has happened to me before. Someone might have seen the bag in the ⓄⓅⒺⓃ locker and moved it somewhere else."

"Let's form groups and look for the bag," Luiza proposed. "We can cover more ground, and maybe we'll find it lying around!"

The ten of them split up into smaller groups and began to search for the bag. They looked in the locker rooms, in the hallways, and in

the stands, but there was no trace of the
BATONS!

Just when she and her friends were about
to give up, Paulina noticed something red
poking out of a trash can at the entrance to
the sports facility.

"Wait!" she said. "Look at this! I
think I may have found what
we've been searching for."

Paulina was right! The
bag was Paulo's, and the
batons were inside.

Is this it?

"But how did it
end up in the trash
can?" Nicky asked,
a puzzled look
on her snout.

"I don't know,"
Paulina replied.

"But one thing is **certain**: It didn't end up there by mistake!"

"Who would do such a terrible thing?" Paulina whispered to herself.

THE TROUBLE CONTINUES

"It was in the **trash**?" Beatrice exclaimed in surprise when Paulina and Nicky told her where they had found the batons. "But who would have put the bag there?"

The Thea Sisters and Bea joined up with the others and gave Paulo the bag. Everyone began chattering about the discovery.

"Maybe the cleaning staff found it somewhere and **thought** it was trash," Nicky guessed.

"Yes, maybe," Pamela agreed. "Sometimes the **answer** to a problem is the **simplest** explanation!"

"Whatever happened, I'm glad we have the batons back," Paulo said. "And we really need to start practice **right away** — we've lost so much time already! We only have a little while before we have to leave the track and let the next team have a turn."

Without another squeak, Beatrice, Vera, Luiza, and Fernanda took their places. The Thea Sisters headed to the first rows of the stands to **WATCH**.

The team had just taken their positions on the track when Paulo's snout clouded over, and he called Bea, Vera, Luiza, and Fernanda back to him. The Thea Sisters walked over to find out what was happening.

"What is it?" Beatrice asked. Paulo was scowling at his stopwatch with a look of frustration.

"My **STOPWATCH** isn't working!" he explained. "The time calculations are off."

"It must be broken," Paulina said.

"It definitely could have chosen a better moment to **break**, though," Pam joked in an attempt to lighten the group's **DARK** mood.

"Unfortunately, this means we can't do the workout I had planned for today," Paulo said with a sigh. "And we don't have much time before the **qualifications**. Why is everything going wrong today?"

"Maybe we can have a longer practice tomorrow to make up for it," Fernanda proposed.

"Yes, that's a good idea," Paulo replied. "Why don't you four go change. I'll put the bag back in the locker, and I'll meet you at the exit to **plan** tomorrow's training session."

Beatrice, Luiza, Vera, and Fernanda **WALKED** toward

the locker rooms to change out of their workout clothes. Meanwhile, Paulo headed toward the office he shared with a few other coaches. The Thea Sisters walked toward the exit, reflecting on the day's events.

"What an unfortunate coincidence," Violet observed. "It's **bad luck** to have the batons go missing on the same day Paulo's stopwatch breaks!"

"I wouldn't call it bad luck," Colette said with a sigh. "Poor Beatrice. She already has enough on her mind."

At that moment, the Thea Sisters heard their friend's squeak behind them.

"Colette, Violet!" Beatrice called from the locker room entrance. "Nicky, Pam, Paulina — **WAIT**!"

Bea sprinted over to her friends and stopped to catch her breath.

"Someone stole Fernanda's and Vera's shoes!" she announced. "While Luiza and I finished changing, they went to get something to drink. They left their bags oᴜtSiⅮe their lockers unattended. When they came back, they realized the bags had been opened — and their shoes had disappeared!"

"But who would have taken their shoes?" Nicky asked in surprise.

"I don't know," Bea replied. "Nothing like this has ever **HAPPENED** before!"

The Thea Sisters tried their best to make their **friend** feel better.

"Don't worry, Bea," Violet comforted her.

"Your team is **strong**; you'll get past this."

The others nodded in agreement.

"We'll help you get to the bottom of this **Mystery**," Paulina said.

There was one thing that was suddenly becoming clear to all the mouselets: There was **NO WAY** the team's troubles were a coincidence!

CLUE!
WHO STOLE VERA'S AND FERNANDA'S RUNNING SHOES? AND WHY? IT SEEMS LIKE SOMEONE REALLY WANTS TO PREVENT THE TEAM FROM TRAINING FOR THE MOUSELYMPICS . . .

GATHERING CLUES

Of course, Paulo was upset when he heard the news. The Thea Sisters hadn't known him long, but they could already tell how **passionate** he was about his coaching, and how important it was to him that his **ATHLETES** had the best opportunities.

"But why would someone have a **problem** with our team?" Paulo wondered. "I don't **understand**!"

"I agree it's a mystery," Pamela admitted. "But it's very clear something **suspicious** is going on. Vera's and Fernanda's shoes couldn't have **disappeared** by themselves!"

But why?

"Maybe we need to ask around," Colette said. "A lot of athletes practice at this facility every day, so there are mice coming and going all the time."

"Good point, Colette," Paulina agreed. "Maybe someone saw something unusual that might be a **clue**."

"That's a great idea!" Beatrice said, smiling at her friends. "I want to help!"

"You're already **so busy**," Violet told her friend gently. Then she turned to Luiza, Vera, Fernanda, and Paulo. "You all have so many other things to think about as you train for the **MOUSELYMPICS**."

"Yes," Colette agreed. "Leave this to us. Tomorrow you five should **TRAIN** as you usually would, and the five of us will launch an investigation."

The next day, the Thea Sisters arrived at

the track with Beatrice very early. Then they left her to train with her team as they set out to interview mice around the **FACILITY**.

The first mouse they encountered was Omar, a member of the cleaning staff.

"Hmm," he said as he thought back over the previous day. "I don't think I noticed anything strange yesterday. I'm sorry."

"Are you sure?" Paulina urged him. She knew that sometimes even a small detail could be helpful in an investigation. "Even something that seemed insignificant at the time . . ."

"Well, there were only two teams training here yesterday," Omar reflected. "Paulo's team and Rodrigo's team. Maybe you could talk to him and his athletes to see if they saw anything **unusual**."

"That's a great idea!" Paulina replied.

"Where can we find them?"

Omar scratched his head.

"I'm not sure," he said. "I don't think they're **TRAINING** here today."

After thanking Omar for his time, the Thea Sisters headed to the snack bar where Vera and Fernanda had gone the day before after

practice had been canceled. There they found a friendly mouse named **Maria** who was happy to help.

"Yes, I was working that day, and I remember those two runners," Maria said, recalling Vera and Fernanda. "They came in here to buy drinks, and then one of them went outside to answer her phone. I think the one who stayed here is named Vera. She was very nice! We chatted a bit about sports. But, I don't know the other's name."

"It's Fernanda," Colette said.

The five friends thanked Maria. As they walked away, Pamela had a **SUDDEN** suspicion.

"Why didn't Fernanda tell us she took a call when she and Vera went to get drinks?" she wondered aloud.

"I was thinking the same thing!" Nicky exclaimed.

"Maybe she just didn't think it was important," Violet said.

"Or maybe she chose not to tell us because she's **hiding** something," Paulina said.

"True," Nicky said thoughtfully. "If she were trying to **SABOTAGE** the team, stealing her own shoes would be a sly move because no one would suspect she would steal her own stuff!"

"But why would Fernanda do something like that?" Colette asked.

"I don't know," Pamela replied. "It doesn't make a lot of **sense**."

"We should just ask her about it," Paulina said confidently. "I think if she's involved, she'll tell us."

"Really?" Violet asked in surprise. "Why would she do that?"

"Well, if all the **MYSTERY BOOKS** I've read

have taught me one thing, it's this: The guilty party almost always REVEALS the truth eventually," Paulina explained. "All the detectives have to do is keep their EYES and ears open as they gather the clues!"

A NEW CHALLENGE

In the days that followed, the Thea Sisters watched Fernanda closely to try to **figure out** if she had been involved in the strange mishaps at the track. But they soon realized that though she wasn't the **friendliest** mouse, she seemed just as **dedicated** to the team as Bea, Luiza, and Vera. It seemed like she wanted to participate in the Mouselympics just as much.

The Thea Sisters

Hmmm...

Who knows...

CLOSED

continued to pay close attention and look for **clues**, but nothing else out of the ordinary happened.

During the days, the **five friends** took long walks around the city or helped Beatrice with her many responsibilities. In the evenings, they met the Oliveira family at the churrascaria for nights full of **delicious** food and good company.

Even though things seemed to be going well, Bea was still worried. One night, the Thea Sisters noticed that Bea's eyes were teary after a **chat** with her parents.

"We have to ask her what's bothering her and see if there's anything we can do to help," Colette said decisively. She and the others were on their way to the **UNIVERSITY** to join Bea, who was finishing up a study session.

"You're right, Coco!" Violet replied.

A moment later, Beatrice emerged from the large medical school building, and they rushed over to **meet** her. It didn't take much to convince Bea to open up to them. In fact, she had been waiting for the right moment to do so.

We need to talk to her!

"You're right," she admitted with a sigh. "I'm sorry if I haven't been much of a fun host. Lately I'm lost in my own thoughts much of the time."

Bea sat down on the steps, and the Thea Sisters gathered close around her.

"This time it's not about the MOUSELYMPIC qualifications," Bea explained. "At least not directly.

CLOSED

"My parents' **CHURRASCARIA** hasn't been as busy as usual. A trendy new restaurant opened nearby a few months ago. At first my parents didn't think the new restaurant would impact their business much. But it turns out that it has. Last night they told me they think they might need to close the churrascaria."

"But how can that be?" Pamela asked. "Everyone loves the restaurant!"

"And it's one of Rio's historic landmarks!" Violet added.

Beatrice nodded *sadly*. "That's true," she said. "It's been such a big part of our family for so long. I can't imagine it closing down. But in order to remain open, business has to pick up. My parents want to organize a party at the churrascaria to get some *publicity* and new customers."

"That sounds like a **great** idea!" Colette exclaimed. "And it will be a lot of fun to organize a party."

"What a great way to advertise to new customers," Paulina added confidently. "I just know it will work."

How can I do it all?

"I really think it could," Beatrice replied. "But I'm **worried** that I won't be able to help planning a big party on top of everything else. I still have my schoolwork and my training. How will I have **time** for it all?"

"I wouldn't worry about that, Bea!" Pamela reassured her. "You don't need to do everything **alone**. You have five friends right here to lend a paw. We would be happy to help."

"Pam's right!" the others agreed.

"I couldn't ask you to do all that work," Beatrice said. "You're supposed to be on vacation."

"It will be fun!" Colette said.

"We would be delighted to help." Pam agreed.

Beatrice smiled. "You five are the

best friends a mouse could ask for!"

TEAM SPIRIT?

Warm rays of sunlight had just begun to light up the Oliveira house. The Thea Sisters were already gathered around the breakfast table when they heard pawsteps approaching.

"She's coming!" Pamela whispered as she set a tea kettle down on the table.

"Oh!" Beatrice exclaimed in **surprise** as she came into the kitchen to find the five mice gathered around. "What are you doing up already? It's still so early!"

"We know you are super busy, but breakfast is the most importnat meal of the day!" Collette said.

"So, we thought having a nice, relaxed breakfast together was the **best** way to begin the busy day that awaits us," Violet explained as she poured Bea a cup of tea. "Weren't we right?"

Beatrice picked up a pastry and smiled at her friends. "What a great idea. Thanks!"

After breakfast, Beatrice dropped the twins off at school like usual. Then she headed to the **LIBRARY** to study, to the **UNIVERSITY** for classes, to the **CHURRASCARIA** to help her parents organize the party, and, finally, to the **track** for running practice. The Thea Sisters tried to keep up with her, but it was tough!

"Are you okay?" Beatrice asked them as

she **SPRINTED** through the streets of Rio de Janeiro from one place to the next.

"Yes!" Pamela replied, panting. "But racing after a track champion isn't easy, Bea . . . You're **TOO FAST**!"

Beatrice slowed down and giggled.

"I train every day in order to get *faster*," she said, "so I should hope that I run faster than you all. Otherwise I'd need to practice more!"

"Luckily, we're almost there," Colette huffed. She pointed at the athletic facility, which was now in sight. "Any more running and I would need a week of rest to recover!"

"You can squeak that again!" Pam said. "I'm going to be one sore mouse tomorrow!"

"I'm going to go *AHEAD*," Bea said as she quickened her step. "I'm already late and I still need to change!"

"We'll meet you there," Nicky said.

The girls **slowed** down and walked toward the track. When they arrived a few minutes later, they expected to find Bea warming up with her teammates. But when they took their places in the stands, they quickly realized that something was **wrong**.

Paulo was nowhere to be found, and Luiza, Fernanda, Vera, and Bea were **ARGUING** about something.

The Thea Sisters hurried down to the track to find out what was happening.

Is everything okay?

"Not again!" Fernanda huffed at Beatrice, who looked mortified. "You're always late for training, and now this! It's not fair to the rest of us who are working hard at this! If you don't want to be on the TEAM, you can just tell us instead of making excuses. We'll find someone to replace you."

Fernanda crossed her arms and glared at Beatrice.

"It's not an excuse!" Beatrice exclaimed. "My sneakers must have fallen out of my bag while I was hurrying to get here."

Bea looked down at her flip-flops in dismay.

"It's not her fault!" Pamela rushed to defend her friend. "It was an accident. It could have happened to anyone! And good luck finding anyone nearly as good as Bea is."

"These sorts of things always seem to happen to Bea," Fernanda said, scowling. "I can't remember the last time she was on time to practice. I keep thinking she's always late because she's looking for a reason to skip training. In fact, maybe Beatrice lost her shoes on purpose. Then she stole mine and Vera's as well!"

"Me?" Beatrice gasped in shock. "How could you **SAY** that?"

Suddenly, Paulo interrupted the argument.

"What's going on here?" he asked sternly. "I don't want to hear any more accusations. You four are supposed to be a TEAM! I'm very disappointed. You all need to take a minute to calm down."

What's going on here?

The Thea Sisters looked at Beatrice. They knew how much their friend cared about her team. Fernanda's and Paulo's words must have been **hurtful**.

"Poor Bea," Violet whispered to Colette. "Fernanda really seems to have a **grudge** against her."

"Yes, you're right," Colette replied softly. "I wonder why."

A STRANGE
ENCOUNTER

After Paulo set the mouselets straight, Bea decided to dash home to grab another pair of sneakers. After all, a true team player doesn't give up easily. The Thea Sisters offered to go with her, but Beatrice assured them that she would be *faster* on her own. Bea gave them a quick wave good-bye and hurried toward the exit.

Colette, Paulina, Violet, Nicky, and Pamela wanted to help Bea out somehow, but they were at a LOSS as to what they could do.

Then, suddenly, **OMAR** ran up to them.

"Do you mice still want to speak with Rodrigo, the coach of the other relay team?" he asked.

"Yes!" Paulina replied without hesitating.

"He's in the sports equipment room right now," Omar said **helpfully**.

"Do you think we did the **right** thing

letting Beatrice go by herself?" Pamela asked, feeling worried. "I know we would have slowed her down a bit, but she seemed so upset and like she really needed a **friend**!"

"I know," Paulina agreed. "I *wish* we could have gone with her, too, but she seemed to need some space. And if we had gone, we might have missed this chance to squeak with Rodrigo!"

"True," Violet agreed. "It's **important** that we get to the bottom of things. He might have useful information to share."

"Look!" Nicky exclaimed. "That must be Rodrigo!"

She pointed to a **sporty-looking** mouse hurrying out of the room Omar had pointed to.

"Rodrigo!" Colette called out.

The mouse stopped and turned.

"**Hi!**" Pamela greeted him. "Sorry to bother you, but we have a quick question."

"Yes?" he replied impatiently. "What is it?"

"We just wanted to ask you about some strange things that have been happening at the track," Nicky pressed. "We're **friends** with Beatrice, one of the —"

"Sorry, I don't have time now!" Rodrigo interrupted her and then *DASHED* off in a hurry.

"Wait!" Colette called after him. He had dropped a **lock** in his hurry to leave, but he didn't slow down. Colette picked it up and put it in her bag.

"**How strange**," Paulina said in surprise.

"And did you see his reaction when I mentioned Beatrice?" Nicky added.

"As soon as I **mentioned** her, he bolted!"

"Either he doesn't like Beatrice or he's hiding something," Paulina said suspiciously.

CLUES!

WHY WOULD A THIEF STEAL SOMETHING AS INEXPENSIVE AS BATONS?

WHO OPENED FERNANDA'S AND VERA'S BAGS AND STOLE THEIR RUNNING SHOES?

WHY DID RODRIGO LEAVE SO QUICKLY AFTER HEARING BEATRICE'S NAME?

EVERY PiECE in iTS PLACE!

That evening after Beatrice's practice, she and the Thea Sisters headed to the churrascaria: The **party** was coming up, and there was so much to do! They needed the event to make a big splash. The mouselets would help Ricardo and Juliana decide on the menu and **organize** some activities. After a very long, productive planning session, a tired Beatrice headed home with the twins and the Thea Sisters.

Beatrice was quiet on the walk home, and as soon as

they returned to the apartment, she helped the twins into their pajamas, tucked them in, and sat down to read them their favorite BEDTIME story.

The Thea Sisters wished them a good night and went to their room to go over the day's **EVENTS**.

"Beatrice seemed quiet tonight, don't you

Once upon a time . . .

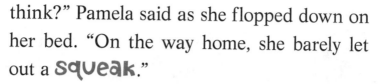

think?" Pamela said as she flopped down on her bed. "On the way home, she barely let out a **squeak**."

"It must be hard for her to balance her studies, her responsibilities at home, and her work at the restaurant," Violet replied. "She has so much on her mind. She must be **exhausted**! I'm sure the last thing she needed today was that little argument with Fernanda and the rest of the team."

"Vi is right. Fernanda was really **unkind** when she accused Bea of not being a team player," Nicky said. "Even though it isn't true, I'm sure Bea was really hurt by it."

"Yes, and the other girls didn't exactly stick up for her," Colette said.

"Sisters, I just had an idea!" Pam **SUDDENLY** burst out, a large smile forming on her snout.

"What is it?" Paulina asked curiously.

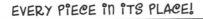

I'll make Bea a sweet treat!

"One remedy for a friend who is down in the snout is a little extra dose of sweetness," Pam explained. "Why don't we wake up early tomorrow and surprise Bea with an even better breakfast than today's? I can bake blueberry banana muffins."

"And I'll make fruit tarts," Violet said.

"**GREAT** idea," Colette said. "I'm in!"

"Then we'd better get to sleep right away!" Pam said.

Colette began her bedtime routine, which she always started by emptying her bag. She put all its contents on her nightstand, including the lock Rodrigo had dropped in his **hurry** to leave the athletic facility.

"What's that?" Paulina asked, curious.

"It fell out of Rodrigo's bag when he left," Colette explained. "I called after him, but he didn't **STOP**. I meant to drop it in the lost-and-found, but I guess I forgot I had it in my bag."

"**Hmmm . . .**" said Paulina. Then suddenly she remembered that Paulo had told them the combination to the lock that had gone **missing** along with the batons. She picked up the lock and turned the wheel to the four numbers:

4 4 0 0 Click

The lock popped open!

"It's Paulo's lock!" Paulina exclaimed.

"Does that mean Rodrigo took the bag with the BATONS?" Violet wondered.

"Probably," Paulina said, nodding.

The pieces to the puzzle were starting to fall into place.

"Rodrigo trains his own team of very talented athletes," Colette pointed out. "His team is probably competing with Beatrice, Vera, Fernanda, and Luiza to qualify for the MOUSELYMPICS."

"If Rodrigo sabotaged the rival team's practice, his athletes would have a better chance of winning!" Nicky agreed. "It must be him, he has so much to gain. I wonder if the whole team is in on it."

"I don't know. We need to tell Beatrice immediately!" Pamela said. They went to find her. But when the Thea Sisters reached the twins' room and poked their heads in, they saw Beatrice asleep in a chair, the BOOK of fairy tales still in her paws. She was so tired she had fallen asleep along with her little brothers!

"I think we can wait until morning," Pamela **whispered** to her friends. "We'll squeak with her first thing!"

Zzzzz . . .

THE MISSING
FRIEND

The next morning, the Thea Sisters were up before the SUN. They were very careful to be as quiet as possible while they scurried around the kitchen making a batch of blueberry banana muffins and fruit tarts. Soon the **warm** treats were out of the oven and cooling on the counter, but there was still no sign of Beatrice.

"Maybe she turned off her alarm clock and fell back asleep like I often do," Violet said. She and her friends sat around the **kitchen** table, wondering where their friend could be.

"What if her alarm clock is **BROKEN**?"

Pamela wondered. "Maybe we should go check on her. Bea would be really upset if she was late to TRAINING again!"

"I'll go see," Colette volunteered. She tiptoed down the hallway and knocked lightly on Bea's door. When there was no reply, she peeked inside. **Beatrice wasn't there!**

"She must have gone out super early!" Nicky said, when Colette shared the news.

How strange . . .

"How strange," Paulina said, perplexed. "It's too early for the **LIBRARY** to be open. I wonder where she went."

"And why she didn't leave a note!" Pam added.

The Thea Sisters decided to investigate. First, they headed to the library. By the time they arrived, the building was just OPENING for the day. But Beatrice wasn't among the students waiting to enter.

"Why don't we try the track?" Colette suggested.

But when the five friends arrived at the athletic facility, it was EMPTY.

"I guess we should head back to the apartment," Paulina proposed. "Maybe Bea

Where's Bea?

She's not here, either!

How strange...

had to run an ERRAND this morning and she's back now."

The Thea Sisters tried to stay calm as they headed through the streets of Rio, but they were worried. It wasn't like Bea not to let them know where she was going. Did she want to be alone? Was she hiding something?

When they got home, the apartment was EMPTY. The twins had a DAY OFF from school, and Bea's parents had taken them to the churrascaria with them.

"Let's try calling her," Violet suggested. But there was no **answer**.

"Maybe she silenced her phone because she doesn't want to talk," Nicky hypothesized.

"Or perhaps she didn't take her phone with her," Violet said.

"That's unlike her," Pamela pointed out. "She never leaves home without her phone and the smartwatch she wears for training."

"Right, the watch!" Paulina repeated as a smile spread across her snout. She headed to the living room and sat down in front of the Oliveira family **computer**. Bea used it to study while her parents used it for their restaurant bookkeeping.

"Bea wears her watch to MONITOR her progress as she runs," Paulina explained. "It's connected to a computer program that keeps track of her in real time. If she's wearing her watch right now, we may be able to track her down!"

The mouselets called Juliana at the churrascaria and asked for permission to use the computer. A few minutes later, Paulina was tapping away at the KEYBOARD.

"There she is!" she exclaimed, pointing to a **BLINKING** red dot on the screen. It was a satellite map of the city, and the dot was moving slowly.

"Are you sure that little dot is **Bea**?" asked Nicky.

Paulina nodded. "If she's wearing her watch, then **Yes**, that's her!"

"Well, then, there's only one thing to do," Pamela said. She headed toward the door. "Let's go **FIND OUT**!"

An Unusual Discovery

Paulina had studied the computer image and realized Bea was at a **sports complex** on the other side of the city. She and Nicky, Colette, Pam, and Violet had to take two buses to get there!

"Maybe Bea went there for a SPECIAL practice," Colette said.

Still, Bea's location seemed **strange**: Why hadn't she told her friends where she was going? And why had she left so early and turned off her phone?

"We're almost there!" Paulina said as she looked at the SCREEN of her phone.

"The field must be pretty close from here."

As soon as the track was within sight,

Colette, Pamela, Paulina, Nicky, and Violet RAN the last bit. When they arrived, they saw Bea immediately: She was stretching on the track along with Vera, Luiza, and Fernanda!

We're almost there!

"What are you doing here?!" Beatrice exclaimed in **surprise** when she saw her friends.

"We were about to ask you the same question!" Colette replied. "We were worried when we didn't see you this morning."

"We tried calling, but when you didn't answer we grew more concerned," Nicky added. "We looked for you everywhere!"

"What are you four doing?" Violet asked.

Beatrice was about to reply when Fernanda cut her off.

"Bea is about to **prove** that she wants to stay on our team," she said, crossing her arms over her chest and glaring at the Thea Sisters. "Lately, she hasn't been much of a TEAM PLAYER."

"And how is she going to prove to you that she cares about the team?" Pam asked, raising an eyebrow.

"By showing that she's a serious athlete!" Fernanda replied. "She should be running her fastest times ever right now. Lately, she's been FALLING BEHIND!"

"And what made you bring Bea all the way out to this track to prove herself?" Colette asked.

"It's quiet at this track; no one ever comes here," Fernanda explained. "She has to show

us that she's good enough to **compete** in the Mouselympics!"

"And you agree with *Fernanda*?" Paulina asked, turning to Vera and Luiza.

The pair lowered their **EYES**.

"The competition is really fierce," Vera said quietly.

We all want to qualify!

"Fernanda isn't the only mouse who wants to *WIN*," Luiza agreed. "We all do."

"Of course," Pam replied. "Bea wants to win, too! But this isn't how you treat a teammate."

Everyone was silent. From the looks on their snouts, it seemed as if

Vera and Luiza knew how unfair their trial was to Bea.

"I'm not an athlete," Colette said, breaking the silence. "But I know what it means to be part of a team. Teammates support one another!"

"Beatrice has a lot going on right now," Paulina pointed out. "Real friends would have helped her, not made things harder for her."

The Thea Sisters' words seemed to sink in.

"Beatrice, I'm sorry," Vera said sincerely. "We haven't been good teammates!"

"I was wrong, too," Bea whispered, hugging Vera tightly. "I should have asked for help instead of trying to do everything on my own."

"NO," Fernanda said firmly. "It's my fault! I was so focused on qualifying for the

Mouselympics, I forgot how much I care about you, Bea. I'm so sorry."

"We may have figured out what's been going on at the track!" Pamela jumped in. "We finally figured out who sabotaged your **practices**."

"Really?!" Bea exclaimed. "Who was it?"

"We'll tell you along the way," Violet explained. "Let's head back so you can all show one another what it means to be a **TEAM**!"

A TRUE TEAM

The morning sun was high in the sky as the city prepared to host the Mouselympics. Banners and flags from the many countries around the world that would soon be competing waved on every corner, and the city seemed to **buzz** with excitement.

The Thea Sisters, Beatrice, Vera, Fernanda, and Luiza hurried through the city. As they dashed through the streets, the mouselets filled the teammates in on what they had discovered.

"Paulo won't believe his ears," Fernanda

squeaked. "I don't think he ever **considered** that his colleague Rodrigo could have been behind everything. He always seemed so nice and helpful! Maybe that was part of his plan."

A few minutes later, the girls found Paulo. They quickly told him what they had discovered: It seemed as though Rodrigo had been trying to **SABOTAGE** their team!

"Rodrigo?" Paulo asked in shock. "Are you **absolutely** sure?"

"Look what we saw fall out of his bag." Paulina showed him the lock Rodrigo had dropped.

"This is **MINE**!" Paulo exclaimed. "I knew Rodrigo really wanted his team to **qualify**, but I didn't think he would try to

hurt my team in order to do it!"

"We can't think of any other **explanation**," Beatrice told her coach.

"Bea's right," Fernanda agreed. "It seems Rodrigo wanted to disrupt our training so his team would have a better chance at **qualifying** for the Mouselympics!"

"I'm going to find Rodrigo so we can get to the bottom of this," Paulo said. Then he disappeared inside the sports facility. A few minutes later, he was back.

"Did you speak with him?" Paulina asked.

Paulo nodded. "You were right," he said sadly. "Rodrigo confessed right away: He said he took the bag from my locker. He was so embarrassed he couldn't even look me in the eye when he told me. I have to go file an official report with the Sports Federation as soon as possible!"

"Does that mean his TEAM will be disqualified?" Nicky asked, a worried look on her snout. "We don't think they had anything to do with his plan."

Paulo hesitated. "I'm not sure," he replied. "Unfortunately, I think that's **possible**."

"But the athletes weren't INVOLVED!"

Beatrice exclaimed. "That doesn't seem **fair** to them."

"True," Vera said. "It was Rodrigo's fault."

It's not right!

"Bea and Vera are right," echoed Fernanda. "They always train hard, and they deserve a chance to qualify."

"We could always **testify** that they had no idea what Rodrigo was doing," Luiza added. "Maybe they'll listen to us!"

Paulo smiled. "I'm proud of you four!" he said. "You clearly understand the real spirit of the sport. Teamwork and loyalty are more important than any victory!"

The Thea Sisters smiled happily at Beatrice, Fernanda, Vera, and Luiza.

Despite the team's many challenges, they were clearly

more united now than ever before!

A BiG PARTY!

Juliana and Ricardo's original idea was to have a party at the churrascaria for the neighbors and new customers.

But thanks to the Thea Sisters, Beatrice's parents decided to completely renovate the restaurant as well! The walls were painted a vibrant yellow, **tablecloths** were replaced, and new decorations, and centerpieces were added to give the churrascaria a *fresh* look. They even printed new munus.

"I don't know how to thank you!" Juliana said to the Thea Sisters. "This place looks *fantastic*!"

No one could believe how much the makeover had improved the churrascaria.

Just a few updates here and there had given the place a bright, modern feel!

"It's even more beautiful than I could have imagined," Ricardo agreed. "I'm squeakless! We couldn't have done this without you five."

"It's been our pleasure!" Nicky replied. "Consider it a way to thank **YOU** and your family for your hospitality and kindness to us!"

"And now we have a special **surprise**," Pam said.

She reached into her pocket and pulled out a photo of a group of musicians. "Samba Saudade!"

"The bossa nova group?" Beatrice asked, confused. "What do you mean?"

"Violet contacted one of the members of the band via email to ask them to play here the day of the party," Pamela explained.

Bossa nova is a style of Brazilian music that originated in Rio de Janeiro and became popular in the late 1950s. It is a combination of samba, traditional Brazilian music, and American-style jazz.

"How wonderful!" Juliana said, covering her mouth with her paw in surprise. "We must spread the word . . . lots of mice from the neighborhood will want to come see them play!"

"We can make some **POSTERS** to hang around the neighborhood," Beatrice suggested.

"Great idea!" Nicky exclaimed. "Let's get to work **RIGHT AWAY**!"

The friends went back to the apartment and immediately began working on a poster design on the computer. A few minutes later, Beatrice's cell phone rang.

"Hi, Fernanda!" she squeaked, recognizing her friend's **number**. "Yes, what is it?"

Beatrice spoke with Fernanda for a few minutes, and when she hung up, the Thea Sisters saw immediately that she was **upset**.

Hi, Fernanda!

"What's wrong?" Paulina asked with concern. "Did something happen?"

"Fernanda was just letting me know that we were assigned a day and time for our qualification race," Beatrice explained. "It's the race that will determine whether we get to compete in the MOUSELYMPICS."

"That's great!" Colette said. "Isn't it?"

"I have a terrible problem," Beatrice explained. "The race happens to be the exact same day and time as the party at the CHURRASCARIA!"

"There must be a solution," Nicky said. "We can't change the date of the race, but maybe there's something else we can do."

"Unfortunately, we can't change the date of the party, either," Colette pointed out. "We've already booked the band and told a lot of mice! If we made a change now, it would be confusing. We would surely lose customers."

"I think there's only one solution," Violet said with a sigh. "Bea is going to have to **MiSS** one of the events!"

What do I do?

A HEAD-CLEARING RUN

It was a very difficult decision for Beatrice. It was more than just choosing between **two things** that she wanted to do. On the one paw, she had the chance to compete in the **MOUSELYMPICS**, a dream come true for any athlete. Beatrice had been training for years for this moment, and it was important to her.

On the other paw were her parents and the **CHURRASCARIA**. Beatrice knew how hard her parents had worked to build the business, and how important the restaurant's success was for the whole family. Beatrice didn't want to **MISS** the party.

Bea also had a feeling her parents didn't

realize she was still training for the Mouselympics. She had promised them she would **focus** on schoolwork, but they thought she had stopped practicing altogether! She wanted to tell them the truth, but she was afraid now it was **TOO LATE**.

The day after she found out the date of the **race**, Beatrice talked it over with the Thea Sisters.

"When I need to make a hard decision, I **shampoo** my hair," Colette said. "Sometimes I even add a snout mask. It really helps me **relax** so I can think more clearly."

"When I'm stressed out, I cook," Pam explained. "That way while I'm reflecting, I'm also making a **yummy** snack!"

The six friends were gathered in the Thea Sisters' room, and they were **trying** to help Bea figure out what to do. They wanted to

help bring a warm **smile** back to their dear friend's snout.

"Bea, what do you usually do when you're having a hard time with something?" Violet asked in an attempt to **help** her friend.

Beatrice smiled timidly.

It's okay, Bea!

What should I do?

What helps you relax?

"I always do the same thing," she replied. "I go for a RUN."

"Then that's exactly what we should do!" Nicky said enthusiastically.

A few seconds later, everyone was lacing up their running shoes.

"We'll never be able to keep your **PACE**, Bea, but we'll go with you for support!" Pamela said.

"That would be great!" Beatrice exclaimed, smiling.

The group headed straight to the track.

"Don't worry," Bea assured her friends as they all took their positions at the starting line. "I left my stopwatch at home, and this isn't a **race**. We're just here to have fun!"

After a quick warm-up, Bea and the Thea Sisters began to jog around the track, breathing in the fresh air and enjoying the time together. About twenty minutes later, Pamela decided to take a break.

"I'm going to go get some **juices** for everyone," she said.

Then she headed inside the sports facility. She was about to go toward the café when she was distracted by some noises coming from a nearby room. She peeked in and saw Omar moving a large box.

"Do you need some **help**?" Pamela offered.

"Sure, thanks!" Omar replied. "I'm just cleaning out this room. The athletic director has plans to remodel it, and I need to get these old trophies cleared out."

Pamela paused and picked up a photo album that was at the top of one of the boxes.

"Is all this stuff really going in the **trash**?" she asked. "It seems sad to throw away photos of former track champions. These might be very **important** to someone."

"You're welcome to take anything you like," Omar said.

Pamela decided to take the photo album with her. She thought Beatrice and her teammates might find it **interesting**.

Pamela returned to the track and showed Bea her find.

"Wow!" Bea said. "Look at these photos of athletes who used to train right here many **years** ago!"

She flipped through the album, showing the Thea Sisters the images.

"**OH, LOOK!**" Paulina said, pointing at a photo of racers leaping over obstacles

Look at this!

placed around the track. "They must have been running a hurdles race."

"Wait a second," Paulina said as she carefully studied one of the pages. "This mouse looks just like your **father**, Bea!"

Beatrice and the Thea Sisters studied the image carefully. It was at least **twenty** years old, and it showed a young athlete who had just won a **medal**.

"He doesn't LOOK just like my father," Bea said. "That IS my father!"

SECRETS REVEALED

The friends studied the photo closely, first at the track and then back at the Oliveira home.

"I wish photos could **squeak**!" Nicky said. "The only way we're going to get more **information** is if we ask your father, Bea."

"But if the mouse in the photo really is my **dad**, there's a reason he's kept this part of his life a **secret** from me," Beatrice said. "I just wish I knew **WHY** he's never told me."

She sat down and **slowly** flipped through the pages one more time. Maybe she had missed something . . . or **someone**. Then suddenly, she spotted him.

"THAT'S FRANCO!" she exclaimed, pointing at the mouse standing next to her father. "He used to be a trainer at the track. It's been many years since he worked there, but sometimes he comes by in the early mornings to walk."

"So we can ask him!" Paulina exclaimed. "Maybe he can help us **understand** what happened all those years ago!"

The next morning, the Thea Sisters and Beatrice went to the sports facility as soon as the sun was up. They were too excited to sleep in. As expected, they found Franco there, **WALKING** around the track.

When Beatrice and the Thea Sisters

approached him, Franco was happy to share details about his years as a **coach**.

"Of course," he said when he saw the picture of himself. "That photo was taken many 𝓎𝑒𝒶𝓇𝓈 ago, but it feels like it was just **yesterday**!"

"And can you tell me who this athlete is?" Beatrice asked, pointing to her father.

"Why, that's Ricardo!" Franco replied. "I would never forget him. He was one of the best athletes I've ever trained!"

Franco told them that Ricardo had been a promising young hurdler. But unfortunately, he hadn't been able to pursue the sports career he had deserved.

"What happened?" Beatrice asked quietly.

"It was really sad," Franco explained. "He hurt his leg pretty badly and was FORCED to give up on his dreams. I'm not sure what happened to him after that. I haven't seen him in **MANY YEARS**!"

"He opened a CHURRASCARIA," Paulina explained. "You must come visit. It's a great restaurant!"

"And he has an amazing family," Colette added, looking at her friend.

"He's a great dad," Beatrice chimed in,

smiling. Thanks to Franco's story, she was beginning to understand her father better. "In fact, he's the most **wonderful** dad a daughter could ever ask for!"

It's really him!

A FAMILY MEETING

Once Beatrice knew the athlete in the photo truly was her **father**, she was eager to learn more. Franco told her all that he remembered about the young Ricardo. From these stories, Beatrice put together a new picture of her dad. He had been a talented, passionate athlete. He had **loved** running and had dreamed of a future in sports. It turned out they had more in common than she ever imagined!

"It must have been tough for your dad to have to give up on his **dreams** after his injury," Colette said sadly.

After their chat with Franco, the friends left the track and went to the **CHURRASCARIA** to find Ricardo. Beatrice wanted to talk to him as soon as possible! To tell the truth, she didn't know what she would say to him. But she knew she had to **tell him** what she had discovered.

But once they arrived at the restaurant and Bea found herself in front of him, it wasn't as easy to talk to her father as Bea had **imagined**.

"What's going on?" her father asked, a look of concern on his snout. He stopped **setting** the tables and pulled up a chair for his daughter. He could tell something was on her mind.

"What do you want to squeak with me about?"

Bea didn't know where to begin. But thanks to the **encouraging** looks from the Thea Sisters, Beatrice was **finally** able to tell her father what she had learned.

"I spoke to Franco at the athletic facility," she finally blurted out. "He **TOLD** me you used to run, and that you were an excellent athlete until your injury."

"I never wanted to keep you from doing something that you love," Ricardo confessed after a few seconds of silence. "But sports

require a lot of time and **work**, and there's no guarantee of success. It only took one accident for all my goals to **go up** in smoke."

"For me, running is a true **passion**," Beatrice explained. "I'm dedicated and I work hard, but I also don't want to be an athlete forever. I want to become a **DOCTOR**. I know how important my schoolwork and studies are.

"But I can't miss the chance to qualify for the **MOUSELYMPICS**. Would you have passed up the chance?"

Ricardo took a deep breath and **smiled**. "You're right," he agreed. "I would have been so happy to have an **opportunity** like that when I was a young athlete!"

"Do you mean you won't be upset if I **RUN** in the qualifying race?" Beatrice asked tentatively.

Ricardo looked at Juliana, who stood just a few steps away and had witnessed the entire scene without squeaking a word. He shook his head.

Oh, Bea . . .

"No, I won't be upset," her father told her.

"Even if it's the same day as the party at the **CHURRASCARIA**?" Bea added.

"As long as you **hurry** here right after," Juliana said, smiling. She gave her daughter a **kiss** on the forehead. "That way we can celebrate your **BIG** race and you can tell us all how it went!"

"We'll make sure of it!" Colette exclaimed. "We'll bring her back here after she becomes a **MOUSELYMPIC** athlete!"

"I only wish we could all be there to watch," Ricardo said, smiling.

THE RACE OF A LIFETIME!

In the days leading up to her race, Beatrice was under a lot of stress. Luckily, she had five supportive friends to help her out!

"Here is your schedule for the next few days," Paulina told her, waving a paper in front of her snout.

"But I already figured out a training schedule with Paulo," Bea said, confused.

"We know," Nicky said. "But if you want to be prepared for the race, you have to do more than just practice . . ."

"You need to relax a bit, too!" Colette finished.

Beatrice read the paper and burst out laughing.

Bea's Schedule

TUESDAY

Beach
volleyball

Trip to the
market

WEDNESDAY

Taste cakes
for party

Diving
competition

THURSDAY

Snout mask
and massage!

"What can I say," she said, smiling. "You five are *fantastic* friends!"

She already felt a little less nervous about the upcoming race.

The last few days before the big event passed in a **flash**. Before Bea knew it, the day of the race had arrived!

Beatrice, Fernanda, Luiza, and Vera arrived at the track bright and early. This was the track they had been training on for years, and they hoped it would bring them

good luck today. The team with the fastest overall time would qualify for the **MOUSELYMPICS**!

"Are you ready?" Colette asked Beatrice. "This is it!"

Beatrice nodded. "I'm ready," she squeaked.

"Whatever the result, you've worked hard and done your best," Violet reminded her.

"To us, you'll always be a **WINNER**!"

"And today we'll be up there **cheering** for you!" Pamela assured her, while Nicky and Paulina held up a large sign of encouragement.

The judges were already in place. There was a judge at the starting **blocks**, one at the finish line, and others were stationed along the track at each point where the teams would pass the BATONS from one runner to the next. A series of whistles let the teams know the race was about to **begin**.

Vera adjusted the starting block and focused her attention completely on the **JUDGE** who was about to start the race.

When the whistle sounded, Vera took off in a flash. With the baton solidly in her paw, she sprinted around the track at top **SPEED**.

Almost as soon as Vera began running, she saw Luiza waiting at the next curve. Luiza started to run, and Vera seemed to fly by as she skillfully passed the baton to Luiza.

Tweeeeeet!

At the next **curve**, Luiza seamlessly passed the baton to Fernanda.

Finally, on the last **curve** of the track, Fernanda raced toward Beatrice and passed the baton to her in a **flash**. Now it was up

I can do it!

to Bea to get to the finish line as quickly as possible!

As Bea gripped the baton in her paw, she knew **THIS WAS IT**!

Beatrice focused on the feeling of her sneakers pounding against the track as she raced toward the finish line, *FASTER* than she had ever run before. Ahead of her, she saw the finish line and **NOTHING ELSE**!

Suddenly, out of the corner of her eye, she glimpsed a **familiar** silhouette on the side of the track. Ricardo had come to **cheer** for her! He wanted to share this special moment with his daughter.

Seeing her father gave Bea a burst of extra energy. In one final **LEAP**, she broke ahead of her opponents and flew across the finish line in **FIRST PLACE.** Amazed, Bea stopped and turned to look behind her. Her teammates ran up to hug her, almost knocking her off her paws!

Hooray!

"We did it!" they yelled happily.

"**YOU WON!**" shouted Ricardo, his eyes sparkling with emotion.

"**Amazing job, Bea!**" the Thea Sisters cheered from the stands.

For Bea and her teammates, competing in the **MOUSELYMPICS** was no longer just a fantasy . . .

IT WAS A DREAM COME TRUE!

HEARTFELT
MEMORIES

A few days before, Beatrice had explained to the Thea Sisters the meaning of *saudade*: a very particular feeling halfway between melancholy and nostalgia. When someone feels saudade, it often means he or she is missing something that hasn't even happened yet.

The Thea Sisters finally understood the **feeling**, now in Juliana and Ricardo's **CHURRASCARIA** for the celebration they had helped plan. Their time in **RiO** wasn't over yet; they were staying to help with the opening ceremony of the **MOUSELYMPICS** and with Beatrice's race.

Even so, the Thea Sisters couldn't help but

feel their hearts were full with joy for what was still to come and sadness over events that had already passed.

Colette, Paulina, Nicky, Pamela, and Violet all looked around the restaurant. The churrascaria was packed with customers, Samba Saudade was playing, and Juliana and Ricardo whirled around, serving their crowd. Meanwhile, Beatrice enjoyed a moment of quiet contemplation after a day full of emotions.

"I think it's the right time," Pamela said as she SEARCHED through her purse.

"Bea!" Colette called their friend over.

"We have something for you," Pamela explained, and she gave Beatrice a small package.

"It's wonderful!" Bea exclaimed as she opened the box. Inside was a necklace with the Mouselympic symbol on it. "How can I ever thank you?"

"It's us who need to thank you," Nicky replied, hugging her friend. "You gave us an unforgettable experience here in Brazil."

"It will always be NEAR your heart," Colette said as she fastened the necklace around Beatrice's neck. "That's the best place to keep your emotions and memories of this special time in your life."

The Thea Sisters and Beatrice clasped paws and embraced once more.

"Here's to amazing adventures!" they cheered happily.